# The Diary

# of

# Robin's Toys

### Ken and Angie Lake

# Clarence the Camel

Published by Sweet Cherry Publishing Limited
53 St. Stephens Road,
Leicester, LE2 1GH
United Kingdom

First Published in the UK in 2013

ISBN: 978-1-78226-025-7
Text: © Ken and Angie Lake 2013
Illustrations: (c) Vishnu Madhav and Joyson Loitongbam,
Creative Books

Title: Clarence the Camel - The Diaries of Robin's Toys

Printed and Bound By Nutech Print Services, India

# Every Toy Has a Story to Tell

Have you ever seen an old toy, perhaps in a cupboard, or in the attic or loft? Have you ever seen how sad they look at car boot sales, unwanted and unloved? Well, look at them closely, because every toy has a story to tell, and the older, the more decrepit, the more scruffy, the more tatty the toy is, the more interesting its story could be. Here are just a few of those toys and their stories.

It was a nice sunny morning, and Robin was looking out of the window. He looked down the street and waited for Grandad's little red car.

Sunday was his treat day, when Grandad took him to the car boot sale. Grandad always gave him 50 pence to spend on a toy, so he was looking forward to it.

It had been sports week at school and Robin thought he would do well in the races.

He had always believed that he could run faster than any of the other children, and he made the mistake of telling them so. But on race day, it didn't quite work out like that.

He had been hoping to go on to the county finals at the end of the summer, so he was really disappointed when he only came fourth. It just wasn't good enough.

His friends had been kind and said, "Better luck next year."

But he knew that luck didn't really come into it; he just wasn't fast enough!

So Robin was still a bit glum as he waited for Grandad to arrive.

Beep, beep! There it was, Grandad's car... Beep, beep!

That made Robin smile, just a little bit.

"Good morning, Robin, how are you today? Did you have a nice week at school?"

"Not really, Grandad. It was sports week and I didn't do as well as I thought I would. Anyway, what sort of week have you had?"

"Oh, not too bad. I have spent a lot of time fixing a shopping basket to Grandma's bike."

"Why is that, Grandad?"

"Well, Robin, apparently Mrs Bagshaw next door has a basket on her bicycle, and your grandma can't be outdone by her. Anyway, let's get to the car boot sale and see if we can find something to cheer you up. Here is your 50 pence; spend it wisely."

"Thank you, Grandad."

Robin knew that his Grandad didn't have much money, but he had a very special gift. It's a secret, though, so please don't tell anyone else.

When Grandad was young he was a magician, and he could cast a spell and make toys talk. Then they would tell him their stories. Well, that's what Grandad said and Robin believed him.

So they always looked for

the interesting toys with lots

to tell, and that's why Robin

took his time to choose the
toys  carefully.

They walked round and round
the stalls looking at the toys.
There were so many of them, all
old and unwanted.

Robin and Grandad had come to know most of the regular stallholders, and they knew that Steady Eddy always had lots of interesting toys.

On this bright Sunday morning, most of the toys looked sad, especially one little camel, and that's what attracted Robin to him.

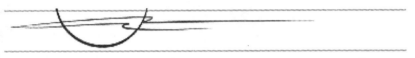

"How much is the camel,
Mr Steady?"

"Clarence the Camel is 50 pence, son. He is a really well-travelled toy. My dad used to work in the oil business in Saudi Arabia and he brought him back for me when I was young.

"Clarence has seen things which you and I can only imagine, so he has to be worth 50 pence. If he could only talk, I bet he would have lots of stories to tell."

Robin smiled at Grandad and gave him a wink. With Grandad's magical powers, they both knew that Clarence would be talking in no time at all.

"Shall I put Clarence in a bag for you?"

When they got back to Grandad's house, he put the kettle on and made some tea.

Then he cut two slices of Grandma's cake. They put Clarence on the kitchen table and Grandad cast his magic spell on him.

"*Little toy, hear this rhyme,*
*Let it take you back in time,*
*Tales of sadness or of glory,*
*Little toy, reveal your story.*"

Then they both settled down and made themselves comfortable, and got ready to listen to Clarence, as he was about to tell them the story of his life.

Clarence looked up, blinked and then smiled.

"Hello! Thank you so much for waking me up, but who are you?"

"My name is Robin, and this is my grandad."

"Oh, nice to meet you both. And what can I do for you?"

"Well, Clarence, we would really like to hear your story. You must have seen some things that we can only dream about."

"Yes, I probably have.
But first of all, do you know
anything about camels?"

"No, not very much."

"Alright, I shall tell you about us.

"Most camels live in deserts and very dry regions where there is not much water. We are really well suited to such places; you see, camels can store moisture and don't need to drink as often as most animals.

"We also have very big feet,
so we don't sink into the sand.
We have lived in these dry

32

places for thousands of years;
it's home to us.

   "We have even adapted to
the terrible dust storms which
can blow the sand around.

   "Because we are so good in
the desert we have been used
to carry things for men, like
tents and cooking pots. That's
why we are called The Ships of
the Desert.

"We also provide our owners with milk and fuel for cooking. To be honest with you both, without camels it would be impossible for men to live in the deserts.

"Now, camels come in two different types. There is the BACTRIAN, which has two humps on its back and comes from the deserts of Central Asia. And the other type is the DROMEDARY; they have just one hump and come from the deserts of Arabia.

"The stories of a
three-humped camel called
HUMPHRY are only rumours,
and part of a very old and not
very funny joke!

*"As you can see, I have one hump, and I grew up in the Eastern Province of Arabia, quite close to a little oasis town called Hofuf.*

"My owner was a very wealthy Arab Sheik (a Sheik is a tribal chief and a very important man). His name was Sheik Yamoney.

"He had bought me at the Camel Sales in Kuwait, because my father had been one of the fastest racing camels in all of Arabia.

"You may think that
Clarence is a very posh name for
a camel; well, my owner got the
name from a doorman at a very
swish hotel in London.

"I was very proud of my name, and when I was growing up I thought that it sort of distinguished me from the rest of the herd.

"It was always my great ambition to become a famous racer, just like my father. You see, racing camels are very important (almost as important as Royal Camels), and worth lots of money.

"As I wandered around in the desert I dreamt of the

future, when I would be famous
as a top racing camel."

"I practised every day by sprinting from one palm tree to another, resting for a bit and then sprinting back again.

*I boasted to all of my friends that one day I would get my picture on the racing page of The Arabian Sun.*

4. Clarence the camel

5. Abdul the camel

"Finally the day came when I was ready for my training to be a great racing camel. A big shiny truck arrived to collect me.

"I strutted proudly up the ramps into the luxury of the truck. All of my friends stood watching; they were so jealous, and I enjoyed the attention.

"The big truck drove through the desert for several hours, and then it stopped. I strutted out into the bright sunlight.

"Where was I? What was this place? It was so beautiful that I couldn't believe my camel eyes. I had arrived at the Racing Camel Training Centre.

*"Everywhere was green; I had been used to a landscape of sand and scrub. What was all that green stuff? Could it all be grass?*

"I had never seen so much grass in my whole life; and there were water sprinklers everywhere, and beautiful palm trees waving in the warm desert breeze.

"I looked over at the luxury stables and the flat sandy areas for race training. This place looked like camel heaven.

"Then I was led off to my own five-star stable, where fresh clean water and very

*special food were waiting for me. I was allowed a whole day of rest and relaxation and being treated like the king of the camels.*

"Early the next morning, just as the sun was rising, I heard a knock on the stable door. The door opened slowly. It was the head trainer, Mr Hassan.

" 'Come on, Clarence, time for some work.'

"I had dreamt of this moment all my life.

53

"Mr Hassan led me out past the stable blocks, past the waving palm trees and onto the training track, where I lined up with five other camels.

"There was a sudden bang and they were all gone. We must have started, I thought,

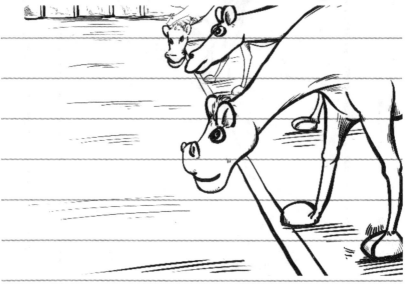

so off I went, as fast as my legs could go.

   "After a few strides I was puffing and panting, and I just couldn't catch up with the others.

"I went back to my stable a
very sad and dejected camel,
but I knew that I could do
better than that the next day.

"The next morning I was ready for the bang, but the others still got away first, and although I tried my best, I just couldn't catch up.

"The walk back to the stable was even worse than the previous day, and I was even sadder than before. But I was determined that the next day I would come first.

"I knew that I could be a winner, and the next day I was going to prove it to everyone.

"I didn't sleep much that
night, even though I had a bed
of soft straw to keep off the
chill of the desert night. The

next morning, I was led to the track again.

"I lined up with the other camels, waiting for the start signal. Bang! We were off;

SURE!

I was going as fast as I could and just about keeping up.

"After a hundred paces they were pulling away from me. I tried to sprint, but my legs wouldn't go any faster.

"I was puffing and panting, but I was falling further behind. I tried as hard as I could, but I just couldn't catch up with the others.

"As I was led back to my stable, I was thinking, Right, I will show them; tomorrow they will eat my dust! I shall prove to

*everyone that I am the fastest*

*camel in Arabia.*

"I had another sleepless night, and in the morning I waited for Mr Hassan to lead me to the training track, but he didn't come.

"I paced up and down the stable, wondering where he had got to. He had never been this late before. Maybe it's a holy day, I thought. Yes, that could

*be it. They are all at the mosque,*
*and we have all got the day off!*

"I waited and waited and waited, and then late in the afternoon Mr Hassan arrived. He slowly opened the stable door and shut it behind him.

"He spoke to me in a serious voice. 'Now, Clarence, I am sorry to have to tell you this, but you are going home.'

" 'What, you mean that I am already good enough to race?'

" 'No, Clarence. I am sorry to have to tell you that you will never be a racing camel, you are just not fast enough.'

"I was totally devastated; all that I had dreamed of was to be a top racing camel, the best in Arabia. I felt ashamed. What would I tell my friends?"

"I had to come to terms with the fact that I was not special; I was just an ordinary camel. This really hurt me, more than you could ever believe.

"The journey back to Hofuf was long and bumpy. Eventually,

I was unloaded back in the desert to join the rest of my herd.

"I was the saddest camel in the whole world. I just couldn't face my friends; I didn't want them to know that I was a complete failure.

"So, instead of going back to the herd, near the town I headed off alone in the opposite direction, into the Empty Quarter.

"This was a vast area of drifting dunes and scrub, and not much else. And it went on forever. Very few people can exist there, and only then with the help of camels.

"I wanted to be alone, and believe me, this was the loneliest place on Earth.

"I wandered for days and days, feeling sorry for myself."

"It was late one evening; the huge red sun was sinking behind

*a perfectly formed sand dune*
*and the temperature was*
*beginning to plummet as it does*
*when the sun goes down.*

*"Suddenly, the desert silence was broken by a strange loud buzzing sound. I recognised the noise, but what was it doing here, miles from anywhere?*

"I knew that the sound was a small aircraft, but the engine wasn't well. It was making a spluttering noise which I hadn't heard before.

"The noise got louder and louder, and then suddenly it stopped. I ran up to the top of the nearest sand dune to get a better look. I could see that the little aeroplane had landed nose first in the sand.

"As I raced over to it, I recognised the crest on the

side of the cockpit; it belonged
to my former owner, Sheik
Yamoney. As I stood staring,
the cockpit canopy slid back
and inside was the Sheik
himself.

'Oh, Clarence, it's you!
Please help me,' he said.

"I was delighted that he recognised me and was overjoyed to see me again.

" 'Can you please take me back to the town? You are the only one who can save my life.'

"I knelt down in the sand so that the Sheik could climb on my back, and we set off for Hofuf.

"I didn't need to be told
where to go, or where the
waterholes were along the way.

This was second nature to a ship of the desert.

"When we eventually got back to the town, the Sheik was so grateful to me for saving his life that he gave me a very special honour. He made me one of the Royal Camels.

"This meant I would be allowed to escort the Princes on trips out into the desert, and teach them the ancient ways of their ancestors.

"I have to tell you, Robin, this was the highest honour that a camel could ever receive. But before I started my royal

duties, I had just enough time to go back to find the herd and tell all of my friends about it.

"I couldn't wait to boast about becoming a Royal Camel! But just before I arrived, I changed my mind.

"Instead, I told them all about my humiliation and my failure at the racing school. I thought that they deserved a chance to laugh at me.

"But they didn't laugh at all. They all told me how much they had missed me and how they felt so sorry it hadn't worked out for me.

"My failures had taught me to think about their feelings and not put them down. I had learned to treat others with dignity and not boast about how clever I thought I was."

"Wow, Clarence, what an amazing story! I had no idea about life in the desert. So what happened after that?"

"Well, Robin, I remained as a Royal Camel for many years. I met lots of very important people and did some wonderful

*things, but eventually, it was*
*time for me to retire, so that's*
*what I did.*

"Then I was sold in a local souk - that's a typical Arabian - market and I was bought by an Englishman who was working in the desert for an oil company.

"He brought me back to England for his little boy, Edward. I am sure you know him; he has a stall at the car boot sale."

"Oh yes, of course, Steady Eddy."

The next Monday morning, Robin went back to school. He hadn't forgotten that he didn't make it into the school's cross-country team, and he really wished  he hadn't boasted to his friends that he would win, but it seemed less important now.

The school bell rang and the teacher came into the classroom. She was making a bit of a fuss, shuffling papers and tutting.

"Alright, everybody, please listen carefully. It seems that the school sports day may have to be cancelled."

A sad "Oh no! " came from the whole class.

"Why does it have to be cancelled, Miss?"

"Well, I am sorry to say that the main organiser has been taken ill and will be off for some time, so without an organiser doing a lot of work, we can't put on the sports day. I am really sorry."

Robin put his hand up.

"Please, Miss, I am not fast
enough to take part in the
races, so may I do the
organising?"

"Robin, that is very kind of you, but there will be lots and lots to do. You will have to make lists of everyone who will be taking part, and then give them all numbers and organise prizes, and get people in place to time the winners, and write down the results and organise some medals. Then there will be refreshments to organise and the local newspaper will want to know the results. There will be so much work to be done."

"That's not a problem. I shall be very happy to do all of that so that my friends can have a really good time and take part in the sports day."

All of the class stood up and clapped and cheered for Robin.

"Robin, it's very nice of you to take on all of that work so that your friends can have a nice day. Alright, class, we should all say a big thank you to Robin. We are very proud of you!"

Suddenly, Robin had forgotten all about not being fast enough to qualify for the race! He had a lot of very important things to do.